Charles J. Holmes

Hokusai

Charles J. Holmes

Hokusai

ISBN/EAN: 9783337361259

Printed in Europe, USA, Canada, Australia, Japan

Cover: Foto ©Andreas Hilbeck / pixelio.de

More available books at **www.hansebooks.com**

HOKUSAI

BY C. J. HOLMES

LONDON MDCCCXCIX
AT THE SIGN OF THE UNICORN

PREFACE

Though Japan has had an important influence upon Western design for more than twenty years, that influence has not hitherto been as uniformly beneficial as might have been expected. Oriental art was first brought to Europe as a commercial speculation. It attracted attention at once by its novelty, and the available specimens, good, bad, and indifferent, were accepted and imitated with little or no discrimination. Thus the showy theatrical prints have a quite undeserved popularity, while the genius of the greater artists of Japan is recognised only by collectors. It is for collectors, too, that the extant literature of the subject has been designed. The present series aims at a wider audience. It is only right, therefore, that the personality of a really great artist such as Hokusai, should be detached from the lesser men with whose work Japanese art is too commonly associated.

The task of a writer who wishes to be essentially practical, can be little more than one of judicious selection. With this intention I have devoted only two chapters to history and biography ; the first to give some idea of Hokusai's relation to his forerunners, the second to show the conditions under which he lived and worked. A third chapter is devoted to Hokusai's prints and drawings. Here I have tried to mention only those which people who are not collectors have a reasonable chance of seeing. For the remainder, Edmond de Goncourt's book, in spite of minor inaccuracies, remains the one authority. The next two chapters deal with Hokusai as the painter of Life and of Landscape.

Special attention is given to Landscape, as it is a province of the artist's genius that will have an important influence on modern painting. Last comes a short note on the leading features of Hokusai's design. This note may seem inadequate, but in the allotted space it was impossible to do more without embarking upon a field of technical discussion that is almost limitless, to the exclusion of matter more pertinent to the aim of the Series. After all, far more can be learned from the prints themselves than from any commentary; and if the reader can be induced to consult Hokusai at first hand, the book will have served its purpose. As I have explained elsewhere, fine Japanese prints photograph badly, so that the little engravings at the end of the volume cannot claim always to reproduce the subtler qualities of their originals. On such a small scale this is impossible; but, so long as the reader remembers that they are only illustrations of the text, he should not find them inadequate.

In common with other students of Japanese art, I am indebted for much historical and bibliographical information to the works of Professor Anderson, Mr. E. F. Strange, Mr. Fenollosa, Herr Von Seidlitz, Mm. Edmond de Goncourt, L. Gonse, and M. Rèvon, the foundations on which all subsequent research must be based. For the materials placed at my disposal by certain personal friends I am still more grateful. I have also to thank Mr. C. H. Shannon for allowing me to reproduce a few of his unique drawings; and Mr. T. S. Moore, Mr. T. B. Lewis, and the authorities of South Kensington Museum, for similar permission in the case of books and prints.

WESTMINSTER, *August* 1898.

vi

LIST OF PLATES

INTRODUCTION

THOSE who have studied the evolution of European painting must have been struck, and perhaps saddened, by the exceeding rarity of supreme pictorial success on a continent which, for the last thousand years, might be thought to have had a monopoly of the world's culture. The intellectual activity of Asia during the same period has seemed little more than a vague rumour, which the political impotence of India and China appears to dissipate finally. To claim a place among the great masters for an Oriental artisan, unrecognised even by the connoisseurs of his own country, may therefore seem to convict the claimant of caprice, if not of wilful ignorance. Those unused to Japanese paintings and colour-prints are apt to pass them by as mere curiosities, interesting perhaps, but only one degree less remote and barbaric than the carved monsters on a Polynesian war-club. The mistake is not unnatural. Our own pictorial formulæ and vehicles have so long been stereotyped by custom that we regard them as absolute laws, from which no deviation is possible. We forget that, in their outward decorative aspect, pictures are strictly limited by ever-changing material conditions, by the surroundings in which they are placed. Architecture being the true base of painting in common with the other arts of design, it follows that the scheme of tone and colour in a good picture is always adapted to a place in some building which the artist has, more or less definitely, in his mind's eye. That for modern painters this building should generally be a large exhibition gallery is not the least of their misfortunes.

Now the architecture of Japan is peculiar, a fact which has

to be borne in mind when we criticise the national style of painting. The whole Archipelago is volcanic, and more or less violent earthquakes are exceedingly common. On more stable soils the energy of other artistic peoples has found effective vent in tall and solid edifices of brick or stone. In such a country these are an absurdity. The inhabitants have solved the difficulty by building light and elastic structures of timber, many of which have proved a match for the shocks of eight or more centuries. Though generally erected with an eye to their part in a scheme of landscape gardening, the temples and important buildings often display great beauty of design and detail. Dwelling-houses, on the other hand, are simple in the extreme —mere frames of wood, walled and divided into rooms by sliding lattices, panels, and screens. Furniture is reduced to a minimum. One or two *kakemono* (the tall "hanging-picture" familiar to collectors), with, perhaps, a single piece of choice porcelain, or lacquer signed by a great craftsman, supply all that is thought necessary in the way of decoration. Where all is so empty and spacious, paintings, being things of comparatively small size, must be striking and lively if the effect of the room is to escape the reproach of tameness. Thus arose the conventions that gave Japanese painting, and through it Japanese colour-printing, the peculiar qualities that make them so distinct from Western design.

Hokusai, in his *Treatise on Colouring* (1848), mentions Dutch oil-painting and Dutch etching, with the criticism—"In Japanese art they render form and colour without aiming at relief; in the European process they seek relief and ocular illusion." He concludes impartially by admitting both points of view. Indeed the Oriental position is not wholly indefensible. The omission of shadow, while it hinders the pictorial treatment of much that is attractive to European eyes, and limits the artist to beautiful form and beautiful colour, has at least one advantage. It absolutely precludes the pretentious realism that would make a picture a kind of sham nature, a deceptive imitation of natural objects that is far commoner among us than we are apt to imagine. In the absence of shadow, a picture can never seem to be anything but the flat expanse of pigment that it actually is, and so keeps its place as a part of the wall surface.

It would be a mistake to suppose that Japanese art attained this harmony with its surroundings all at once. In its origin it is wholly derivative, since, for centuries, the island painters did nothing that was not an imitation of the much earlier work of the Chinese and Coreans. Thus to view their achievement in true perspective, we must first examine that of the mainland.

Were we to trust tradition, we should have to believe that art was flourishing in China and Corea long before the Christian era. No paintings, however, are said to survive that are older than the eighth century A.D., the period of the great Wu Taotsz, whose fame is perpetuated by a few works of doubtful authenticity and many fantastic legends. That relating to his end is a fair specimen of them. It is said that he was commissioned by the Emperor to decorate a room in the palace at Pekin. Concealing himself and his work by curtains, Wu Taotsz laboured in solitude for many months. At last the Emperor was summoned to view the completed painting : the curtains were drawn aside, and he was shown a picture of a palace, with splendid gardens behind it. Filled with admiration, he expressed his regret that he could never possess the reality. Wu Taotsz answered by walking up to a door in the foreground of the picture, which he opened, and, turning, invited the Emperor to follow him. As the artist spoke from within the doorway the door suddenly closed upon him, and immediately the whole painting vanished, leaving the Emperor face to face with a blank wall.

Wu Taotsz was followed by generation after generation of excellent painters, and it was not until the end of the fourteenth century that the artistic genius of the Chinese began to show signs of exhaustion, while a hundred years later vigour and originality survived only in the porcelain factories. The art of the Corean peninsula either started earlier than that of the mainland, or developed more rapidly. Whatever the period of its growth its excellence was shortlived, for by the time that Japan was turning its attention to pictures, Corea had ceased to possess a living art, and was content to export the productions of China.

To those unacquainted with the history of Mongol civilisation the sight of even the few specimens of Chinese and Corean painting in the British Museum will come as a revelation, combining as they do an extraordinary vigour and naturalness, with

3

a breadth of mass, a delicacy of handling, and a mastery of cool colour, that remind one of Andrea del Castagno or Paolo Uccello. Only in the period of decline do we come across jagged outlines and crowded contortion ; the early work is as severe and simple as was the Memphite art of Egypt.

When China was prosperous and civilised, and while Corean art was reaching its climax, the Japanese were still barbarians. This composite race—a blend of Malay, Chinese, and Corean elements—displaced the previous settlers, the hairy Ainu, some time before the Christian era. Under the influence of the arts and sciences that reached them from the mainland by way of Corea, they emerged slowly from a savage condition and began to develop a marked taste for industrial and pictorial design. Not to go into historical detail, it will be sufficient to say that as far as painting is concerned, three separate traditions may be traced in Japanese work. Two of these are of considerable antiquity, but are almost entirely borrowed from the art of the continent ; while the third is perhaps more nearly a national product, and, with all its failings, had at least the merit of toler- ance, a merit which enabled it to father the great art of the eighteenth and nineteenth centuries.

The first painting that came to Japan seems to have been the hieratic art of the Buddhist priests, splendid in colour and majestic in sentiment, but so conservative that it has lasted to our own time with comparatively little change. Its practitioners were chiefly skilful copyists who had only a moderate influence on the work of their contemporaries in the other fields of practical art.

Chinese secular art did not become fashionable till a much later period, though the paintings of the mainland must have been imported from the earliest times. The tradition pro- duced no really individual masters before the fifteenth century, when the germ of the school afterwards known as Kano took root. The painters of the Kano school, like their Chinese pre- decessors, worked most frequently in black and white, aiming at a semi-naturalistic treatment of landscapes, animals, and figures modified by the capabilities of the decisive brush stroke used for writing Chinese characters. Though the progress of the school was hindered by too strict adherence to traditional methods and subjects, the freshness and vigour of its great masters are the real

4

backbone of the finest period of Japanese art. No influence is more prominent in the work of Hokusai's maturity than that of the square forcible handling of the Kano painters, indeed their great humorist Itcho seems actually to anticipate the modern master in his lighter vein.

The third school, known first as Yamato and later as Tosa, did not come into prominence till after the great civil wars which devastated Japan in the twelfth century. The Japanese themselves regard it as a national product, and to a certain degree they are right. Tosa painting, however, is not an original discovery so much as a combination of several quite distinct elements ; and, as the school laid the foundations of the section of Japanese art with which we are at present concerned, it deserves more than a passing notice. Though its origin is still uncertain, it would appear from similarities of method and composition that the school was in the beginning a secular offshoot of the hieratic Buddhist art,—a substitution of courtiers and heroes for hermits and celestial personages. On to this stem was grafted, when or how we do not know, the delicacy and prettiness of Persian miniature painting. The outlook of the school was further widened by an occasional fashion for imitating the methods of Chinese artists, and under this influence its best work was done. The Chinese tradition instils a fresh vigour and naturalism into a style of painting that was too often content with bright gaudy colour, absurd conventional clouds, and faces stippled into doll-like inanity. Thus it is that, coupled with scenes from history and court life, we find really beautiful paintings of birds and flowers. It was not till late in the sixteenth century that a Tosa painter, Matahei, broke through the traditions of aristocratic exclusiveness to paint the everyday life around him, and so found the school of " passing-world pictures" (Ukiyo-yé), which produced the great colour-printers of the eighteenth and nineteenth centuries.

Wood-engraving had been practised in Japan from an early period, but had remained barbaric in comparison with Chinese work, until the demand for Ukiyo-yé prints came as a stimulus. The method of cutting was the same as that employed in Europe till the beginning of the present century. The design, transferred to thin tracing-paper, was pasted on to the face of the wood block, and the white spaces hollowed out with a knife and small gouges. The wood, usually that of the cherry-tree, was not hard, and was cut along the grain instead of across the end of it, as is the case with boxwood blocks. No press was used for printing, but the primitive substitute could turn out very perfect work in capable hands, and Japanese hands are usually capable. After the block had been inked, a sheet of damp paper was laid upon it, and the back of the paper was then rubbed with a flat rubber till the impression was uniformly transferred. Where more than one block was employed, as in colour-printing, the subsequent impressions were registered by marks made at the corners of the paper.

Matahei's designs were not apparently engraved, but he was followed by three designers of the highest merit,—Moronobu, Masanobu, and Sukenobu,—whose work gained an extensive popularity among the lower classes by skilful reproduction, though as yet the prints were restricted to black and white, colour being occasionally added by hand. Though the hand-colouring was often exceedingly skilful, it was discarded early in the eighteenth century, when the discovery of printing colours from a second block was made by Kiyonobu. His successors, Harunobu and Koriusai, increased the number of blocks to seven or eight, and produced colour effects that in boldness and subtlety were never surpassed by the later artists. Shunsho carried the pyramidal Tosa composition to perfection in his book of famous beauties; Kiyonaga introduced processional arrangements, and a realism of facial expression unknown till his time; Utamaro practically confined himself to the fair ladies of the Yoshiwara, whose robes and gestures were combined and recombined in a thousand elaborate harmonies; while Toyokuni gained an enormous vogue as the painter of the stage, whose melodrama lost nothing of its extravagance in his hands.

A brief survey of the surroundings of Hokusai's youth would show us the classical Kano and Tosa schools sinking in steady decline at the courts of Yedo and Kioto, while everywhere in the streets of the northern capital cheap coloured engravings of fashionable beauties and fashionable actors had as ready a sale as their modern photographic successors. The enthusiasm of the Japanese people for the loveliness of nature created a market for volumes of birds and flowers, as well as guide-books with views

6

of show-places; their popular novels were crammed with illustrations of the astonishing adventures upon which the characters chanced; fêtes and occasions of ceremony were commemorated by elaborate picture-cards; even the splendid painted *kakemono* of the wealthy had their counterparts in the long colour-prints that hung in the houses of the poor. Thus, while the nobles hoarded their collections of classical paintings, and patronised its effete living followers, the vast majority of the people, the merchants and artisans, had a flourishing art that, in spite of the contempt with which it was regarded by the courtier-connoisseurs of the day, had accumulated a tradition of its own, and in its most exquisite manifestations had already shown a ripeness that was perilously near to decay. The truth is that the Ukiyo-ye art was itself based on an old convention, from which during the eighteenth century it was never wholly able to get free. The genius of Harunobu and Outamaro, though it found new beauties in that convention, only succeeded in the end in making its limitations more apparent than ever; nor could the ruder force of Kiyonaga or Toyokuni lend any permanent help. In fact, by the end of the eighteenth century the perfection of colour and design that had characterised popular painting was already become a thing of the past. Japanese art could only be saved by an absolute revolution, and it is not the least of Hokusai's merits that he had the strength of mind to defy long-continued prejudice and poverty for the sake of nature and life.

In the autumn of 1760, when Hogarth had just had his *Sigismunda* thrown on his hands by Sir Richard Grosvenor, a child was born in a humble suburb of Yedo whose place in the world's art was destined to be at least no less important than that of the English painter of life and character. His parents were of the artisan class; the father a maker of metal mirrors to the court of the Shogun, the mother a member of a family that was not without celebrity in its time, but had lighted upon evil days. Her grandfather had been a retainer of the courtier Kira, in whose defence he had fallen by the hand of one of the forty-seven Ronins during the midnight attack which was the climax of that tragic episode of seventeenth-century Japan. The vassal's family had been involved in the ruin that overtook the house of his master, so that in the next century it was not strange that his granddaughter should have married a workman. Perhaps to this soldier ancestor we may trace the pride and independence that characterised Hokusai all his life, just as the employment of his father—for Japanese mirrors are decorated on the back as well as polished on the face—might be supposed to influence the child's tastes and capacity in the direction of art.

Possibly because he was not an only son, he left home when thirteen or fourteen to be apprenticed to an engraver. Though he did not remain at this trade for more than four years, the experience thus gained must have been exceedingly useful to him in after life, when he had to direct the men who were cutting his own work. Some letters on this point to his publishers are not without interest. In one, dated 1836, we read: "I warn the engraver not to add an eyeball underneath

8

when I don't draw one. As to the noses; these two noses are mine (here he draws a nose in front and in profile). Those they generally engrave are the noses of Utagawa (Toyokuni), which I do not like at all." Several prints actually engraved by Hokusai are still preserved. At the age of eighteen he left this employment to join the school of the great designer, Shunsho, whose colour - prints are among the treasures of modern collectors, where he became an apt imitator of his master's style. His originality, however, could not long be suppressed. An enthusiasm for the vigorous black and white work of the Kano school irritated the old professor, whose dainty art aimed at very different ideals. At last, in 1786, a quarrel over the painting of a shop sign resulted in the expulsion of the disobedient pupil. No doubt such an inquisitive, unconventional scholar must have sadly perplexed a master who had long been regarded, and quite rightly, as one of the leaders of the popular school. Yet in those eight years spent under Shunsho's guidance the younger man must have learned all that was to be learned from Ukiyo-yé art, and no further advance was possible for him until he had gained his freedom.

Thus, at the age of twenty-six, Hokusai was cast adrift upon the world to try to make a living by illustrating comic books, and even writing them. He was attracted for a time by Tosa painting, and worked in imitation of it; but, work as he might, he was unable to make a livelihood. At last in despair he gave up art and turned hawker, selling at first red pepper and then almanacs. One day as he was crying these latter in the street his former master, Shunsho, happened to come along. The pride of Hokusai would not allow him to stoop to begging, so he plunged into the crowd to avoid recognition. After some months of misery an unexpected and well-paid commission to paint a flag aroused hope in him once more. Working early and late he succeeded in executing illustrations to a number of novels, and designed many *surimono*—the dainty cards used for festive occasions—with gradually increasing reputation. It was about this time that he learned, or rather came in contact with, the rules of perspective, and began to catch something of the grandeur of the early art of China.

In the spring of 1804 he made a popular hit by painting a

9

colossal figure in the court of one of the Yedo temples. On a sheet of paper more than eighteen yards long and eleven yards wide, with brooms, tubs of water, and tubs of ink, he worked in the presence of a wondering crowd, sweeping the pigment this way and that. Only by scaling the temple roof could the people view the bust of a famous saint in its entirety. "The arch of the mouth was like a gate through which a horse could have passed ; a man could have sat down in one of the eyes." Hokusai followed up this triumph by painting, on a colossal scale, a horse, the fat god Hotei, and the seven gods of good luck. At the same time, to show the range of his powers, he made microscopic drawings on grains of wheat or rice, and sketched upside down, with an egg, a bottle, or a wine measure. These tricks gained him such a reputation that he was commanded to draw before the Shogun, an honour almost without precedent for a painter of the artisan class. Here he created a sensation by painting the feet of a cock and letting it walk about in the wet colour spread on his paper, till the result was a blue river covered with the floating leaves of the red maple.

In 1807 his connection and squabbles with Bakin, the famous novelist, began. They first collaborated on a book, *The Hundred and Eight Heroes*, which Bakin translated from the Chinese, while Hokusai furnished the pictures. The connection lasted about four years, and was dissolved by an unusually violent quarrel. The pair seem indeed to have been ill-matched. Bakin, serious, distant, absorbed in his literary studies, possibly a bit of a pedant, was no companion for the quick capricious artist. Hokusai's first acquaintance with the actor Baïko was equally characteristic. Baïko, who was especially famous for his manner of playing ghosts, one day sent to ask Hokusai to draw him a new kind of phantom. No reply came, so Baïko called in person. He found the painter in a room so filthy that he had to spread out a rug he had prudently brought with him before he could sit down. To his attempts at polite conversation, and his remarks about the weather, Hokusai made no answer, but remained seated without even turning his head, till at last Baïko had to retire angry and unsuccessful. In a few days he returned with humble apologies, was well received, and from that time forward the two were friends.

In 1817 Hokusai went to Nagoya for six months, staying

in the house of a pupil. Here he repeated the *tour-de-force* that had gained him so great a reputation at Yedo, by painting a colossal figure, in the presence of a crowd of spectators, on a sheet of paper so large that the design could only be shown by hoisting it on to a scaffolding with ropes. More important, however, than this advertisement of his dexterity, was the publication of the first volume of the *Mangwa*, which, according to the latest authority, appeared at this time. The word has been variously translated by such expressions as "various sketches," "spontaneous sketches," "rough sketches," "casual sketches," and so on. The exact meaning is ambiguous even for cultured Japanese, so that it is unnecessary to discuss the matter further here. This volume was the first of the famous series of fifteen which contains so much of the artist's best work.

In 1818 he continued his travels, visiting Osaka and Kioto before returning to Yedo. It would seem that in the ancient capital of the Mikado, Hokusai met with but moderate success. The place was the headquarters of the classical schools of painting, and its refined connoisseurs would recognise but little merit even in the best productions of the popular art. Ten years later, when nearly seventy years old, he was attacked by paralysis, but cured himself with a Chinese recipe that he found in an old book. This recipe for boiling lemons in *saké* (rice-spirit) is still extant, with drawings by Hokusai of the lemon, the manner of cutting it, and the earthen pipkin in which the mixture is to be cooked. Whatever the merits of the medicine, the old artist was thoroughly cured, for it was about this time that he produced the three sets of large colour-prints which are, perhaps, his most important works, the *Waterfalls*, the *Bridges*, and the *Thirty-six Views of Fuji*. It is possibly owing to the misfortunes of the following years that these series seem to be incomplete. Certainly Hokusai had good reasons for not undertaking any commissions that did not bring in ready money, for in the winter of 1834 he had to fly from Yedo and live in hiding at Uraga under an assumed name. The reason of this flight is uncertain, except that it was caused by the misdoings of a grandson. A letter to his publishers explains the measures taken for the reformation of the scapegrace; the purchase of a fish shop, and the provision of a wife "who will arrive in a few days"—at Hokusai's expense.

When writing from Uraga he would not give his address, though he suffered great privations; and when important business recalled him to Yedo, he visited the capital secretly.

It was not till 1836 that he was free to return safely; but the return came at an unpropitious time. The country was devastated by a terrible famine, and Hokusai found that the ordinary demand for art had ceased. To live he was compelled to work day and night, turning out quantities of drawings whose chief recommendation to the public was their cheapness. At last he was reduced to such straits that he had to eke out a precarious existence on handfuls of rice, gained by exhibitions of his manual dexterity. In the following year his patience was again severely tried by a fire that burned his house and all his drawings. Only his brushes were saved; and the poor old man had to keep more constantly than ever to his work, both as a consolation in his troubles and as means of avoiding starvation. Year after year he went on designing with undiminished power and activity; but though he never emerged from the state of chronic poverty that had surrounded him all his life, he never seems to have been again threatened by positive want. Certainly in old age he lost nothing of his skill and little of his cheerfulness, if we may judge from a letter written to a friend during his fatal illness in 1849.

"King Yemma (the Japanese Pluto) being very old is retiring from business, so he has built a pretty country house, and asks me to go and paint a *kakemono* for him. I am thus obliged to leave, and, when I leave, shall carry my drawings with me. I am going to take a room at the corner of Hell St., and shall be happy to see you whenever you pass that way.   Hokusai."

On his deathbed he murmured, "If Heaven could only grant me ten more years!" Then a moment after, when he realised that the end had come, "If Heaven had only granted me five more years I could have become a real painter." With this rather unreasonable regret on his lips Hokusai died on 10th May 1849, in his ninetieth year. His humble tombstone, black and neglected, may still be seen among the pines and cherry-trees of a monastery garden in the Asakusa suburb. In front it bears the inscription:

"Tomb of Gwakio Rojin Manji" (the old man mad about drawing); on one side a list of family names, on the other a poem which the artist, in accordance with national custom, composed during his last hours: "My soul, turned will-o'-the-wisp, can come and go at ease over the summer fields."

Hokusai was twice married, and had five children, two sons and three daughters. The eldest son was a scamp, who inherited the mirror-making business, and was a cause of endless trouble to his father. The younger became a petty official with a taste for poetry. His eldest daughter married her father's pupil Shigenobu, and, before she was divorced from her husband, became the mother of the child whose excesses made it necessary for Hokusai to go into hiding at Uraga. Another daughter died in youth. The youngest, Oyei, married a painter; but her independent spirit led to a speedy divorce, and she returned home to be for many years the devoted companion of her father, whom she did not long survive.

Theirs must have been a curious household, judging from the contemporary accounts that have come down to us. In the middle of the studio floor stood a square brazier containing a few lumps of charcoal. Hokusai, with an old counterpane thrown over his shoulders, sat leaning over his work-table with his back to this poor fire. All around was litter and dirt. The daughter, a skilful artist, with a reputation for fortune-telling, sat working near her father, receiving strangers as best she could in the absence of all the customary means of showing politeness, and fetching food, as required, from a neighbouring shop. Her portrait of Hokusai when about eighty years old forms the frontispiece of De Goncourt's book. When the house got quite unbearably filthy, the pair did not clean it, but hired another. Hokusai thus changed his abode no less than ninety-three times in the course of his life.

In spite of the enormous mass of his work, he remained poor, though he had no expensive habits, no love for wine or gay company, though he lived on the simplest food, though his clothes and furniture were those of an absolute pauper. Yet, though an ascetic by habit, he was by no means intolerant. In his preface to *Cooking at a Moment's Notice* (1805) he writes: " If there be a moralist who has said that at the first cup it is the man who drinks the *saké*, at the second it is the *saké* that drinks the *saké*, and at the third it is the *saké* that drinks the man, there are others less severe, who declare that there is no limit to *saké* drinking, so long as it brings no disorder with it." The truth is, he cared for nothing but his art, and grudged even the time necessary to open the packets of money he received in payment for his drawings. He kept these packets lying by his table. When a tradesman called with a bill, the artist handed him a packet of money without a word, and continued drawing. The tradesman went off and opened his packet. Sometimes he found the amount inside was many times that of the bill ; in that case he held his tongue. If the money was insufficient, he went back and demanded more. No wonder that Hokusai was always a poor man ! His devotion to his art made him proud and inaccessible to those who came to buy his drawings without showing him proper deference ; but many stories are told of his kindness to children, and of his behaving with great delicacy of feeling under trying circumstances. Though his artistic reputation among his own class was enormous, and had even spread to the Shogunal court, he was only known by sight to his intimate friends. There is a well-known story of his spending the evening with three strangers. The party on breaking up could only find a common, unpainted lantern to light them home. It was jestingly suggested that this should be painted. Hokusai, taking a brush, covered the surface rapidly with figures, till one of his companions innocently remarked, " You seem to have some talent for drawing."

Poverty, and even dirt, are not rare accompaniments of genius, but it *is* rare to find a great artist living for nearly a century among the working-classes, his chief customers, to whom in life he was known mainly for his power of drawing in odd ways, such as making pictures out of casual blots of ink, and by whom in death he was immediately forgotten, and yet all the while, among these mean surroundings and ignorant companions, having the courage to adhere firmly to the high ideals he had conceived. Hokusai's own words from his preface to the *Hundred Views of Fuji* are the best evidence of his spirit.

" From the age of six I had a mania for drawing the forms of things. By the time I was fifty I had published an infinity of designs; but all I have produced before the age of seventy is not worth taking into account. At seventy-three I have learned a little about the real structure of nature, of animals, plants, trees, birds, fishes, and insects. In consequence, when I am eighty, I shall have made still more progress; at ninety I shall penetrate the mystery of things; at a hundred I shall certainly have reached a marvellous stage; and when I am a hundred and ten, everything I do, be it but a dot or a line, will be alive. I beg those who live as long as I to see if I do not keep my word.

"Written at the age of seventy-five by me, once Hokusai, to-day Gwakio Rojin, the old man mad about drawing."

Except his daughter, Oyei, Hokusai had no pupils in the ordinary sense of the word, but he had followers who were able to catch something of his manner. Of these his son-in-law Shigenobu was the earliest; but his mature style was more closely imitated by Hokkei, a fishmonger turned artist (and a graceful artist, too), who taught Gakutei the celebrated designer of *surimonos*, and Hokuba, whose book illustrations show a genuine appreciation of Hokusai's dexterity, but lack his spirit and insight. The remaining artists who directly imitated Hokusai need not be taken into account, but three other painters of distinct originality owe much to his influence. Of these the roué Keisai Yeisen and the genial Kiosai, a modern in point of date (he died only a few years ago), display other influences so strongly that their works are not likely to be confused with those of their great predecessor. The third, Yosai, a classical artist of extraordinary power and delicacy, whose chief work is a series of portraits of the great personages of early Japan, owes most of his merit to the fact that he had the sense to combine with the grace and dignity of the Tosa tradition in which he was nurtured, much of the vigour and life that inspired the great master of the popular school. Nevertheless, if we seek to trace the influence of Hokusai, we shall not find its clearest evidences in such work as this, any more than we can lay at his door the utter decay into which the Tosa, Buddhist, and Kano schools have fallen. It is on the work of the Japanese artisans, the flowers, the figures, the landscapes, that decorate the things of everyday use, the pottery, the bronze, the lacquer, the *netsukés*, that the great master of the popular school has left the most enduring impression.   That these are mere articles of commerce, that the impulse that first gave them life has long departed, matters but little.   We recognise their inferiority only when we track the spring of their inspiration to the fountain-head, where any loss that we may feel is more than compensated.

HOKUSAI'S PRINTS AND DRAWINGS

THE student of Hokusai's work is confronted at once with two difficulties — the enormous bulk of his output, and the practical impossibility of looking at more than a fraction even of the small proportion of his prints and drawings that have reached Europe. Hokusai, as we have seen, lived to his ninetieth year, and for the greater part of his life did nothing but draw. The latest catalogue makes him the illustrator of nearly a hundred and sixty different publications, many of them comprising a number of volumes. As the volumes contain on an average fifty pages apiece, each with its illustration, the quantity of his engraved work alone almost defies computation. In addition to this enormous mass of prints, we have to reckon with the studies for these compositions, as well as the innumerable random sketches made to please his own fancy or that of a customer, and with the more elaborate paintings, of which only a limited number have ever been exported. We must always remember, too, that Hokusai, though popular with the lower classes, was hardly known, even by name, to amateurs of position, except perhaps in his native Yedo. His drawings and prints were not usually bought or kept by the wealthy. They were the ephemeral amusement of artisans and shopkeepers, and were lost or thrown aside when they had served their immediate purpose. If, a century hence, our public libraries had been destroyed, and any intelligent Japanese were to discover supreme merit in the drawings of some popular illustrator of one of the halfpenny comic papers of to-day, he would have nearly as much difficulty in forming a representative collection of the work he admired as we have in the case of Hokusai. Though a number of his prints in very varied degrees of perfection are not uncommon, his drawings and paintings are for the most part inaccessible to the general public, remaining as they do in the hands of a few collectors. Thus, while the one existing *catalogue raisonné*, the work of M. Edmond de Goncourt, is by no means complete or invariably accurate, the wonder is that it could ever have been compiled at all. In the few pages here available nothing of the kind can be attempted. All that is possible is to indicate the sections into which Hokusai's work naturally divides, and to discuss only what there is a reasonable chance of seeing.

It will be best to speak of the prints before the drawings, because they are more generally accessible, and more characteristic of the artist's whole purpose. Luckily a chronological arrangement is not only convenient but natural, since, as indicated by the artist's own words, the work done in the first fifty years of his life—that is, up to the year 1810—is quite distinct from that of the last forty. On this basis the engraved work may be classified as follows :—

(*a*) All work done up to 1810—Novels, *surimonos*, and the Views of Yedo.

(*b*) The books of sketches—The *Mangwa*, the *Gwafu*, and their companions, with the *Hundred Views of Fuji*.

(*c*) The books of legendary subjects in the Chinese manner.

(*d*) The large sets of plates, the *Thirty-six Views of Fuji*, the *Bridges*, the *Waterfalls*, etc.

As we have seen, Hokusai began his art education under the eyes of Shunsho. His prints of this period would pass for those of his master ; but his work soon after leaving the school is so unlike that of the older man that one is not surprised at their quarrel. Shunsho's ladies are short and plump ; Hokusai's are as tall and slender as those of Utamaro. Shunsho's colour is a delicate harmony of pink, grey, yellow, and pale green ; Hokusai uses a powerful green, a warm brown, and occasionally strong blues and definite crimson, which are not attuned so easily. The drawing of the younger man is already exquisitely refined, as we can see from the *surimono*, which are more carefully engraved and printed than the picture-books. Indeed these dainty little works, which are, alas ! only too rare, represent Hokusai's early work at its best ; just as in the novels, from the intrusion of the text into the page and from dependence on the subject-matter of the

18

story, it is seen at its very worst. These *surimonos* are interesting, too, as evidence of the strong hold that the Tosa miniature painting had upon Hokusai when he started as an independent designer, though later his plates of the play of the Forty-seven Ronins show that he had not forgotten the forcible Ukiyo-yé art in which he was trained. This series appeared in 1802 ; but from the three sets of Yedo views that appeared about the same time, it is evident that his horizon was rapidly widening.

In 1796 he had come in contact with the rules of perspective through a fellow-countryman, Shiba Gokan, who had studied a Dutch book on the subject ; while it is evident from the *Promenade of the Eastern Capital*, published in black at the end of 1799, and in colour in 1802, that he had been looking carefully at the popular guide-books illustrated in the Chinese style. Possibly it was thus that he was led to appreciate the great art of the mainland, with its vigorous if mannered naturalism, that was to be an increasingly prominent influence in his drawing. During the next four years he made enormous progress, and *The Streams of the Sumida River*, published in 1804, looks like the work of another hand. The pictures in the earlier book are broken up by bars and streamers of conventional pink clouds ; the figures are for the most part too numerous and too tiny, the landscapes wearisome with excess of detail. Only here and there does some more successful design—a bridge packed with a struggling crowd, or a wide plain under snow—give some hint of greatness. The *Sumida River* is full of delightful animated groups, no longer mere dots in a fantastic panorama, but really important features in the design ; while in the landscapes the barred clouds are gone, and only so much scenery is introduced as in it make the whole effective and coherent. In the same way, though the figures remain conventional in their tallness, their actions are no longer conventional (Pl. I.). The naturalness, which was the backbone of the Chinese tradition, was beginning to produce its effect, and the absolute freedom of the *Mangwa*, revolutionary as it seemed to the artist's contemporaries, was really only one more step in a regular process of evolution.

The *Mangwa* is a series of volumes of sketches of all kinds of subjects. As the dates of the appearance of the earlier part of the series are uncertain, it is impossible to say more than that internal evidences point to the series having started some years before 1817, the latest date proposed. As odd volumes of the *Mangwa* are not uncommon, a short description of the contents of each may be useful to chance purchasers, as well as evidence of the ground covered by Hokusai in his search for perfection. It should be remembered that Japanese volumes are read the reverse way to European books.

1. Children, gods, priests, fishermen, acrobats, workmen, ladies at their toilet, men sleeping, praying, walking, animals real and imaginary, birds, insects, plants, fish, mountains, ships, grasses, trees, buildings, waterfalls.
2. The phœnix, dragons, gods, saints, workmen, women and men variously engaged, masks, utensils, rustic steps and stones for rockeries, landscapes, flowers, birds, animals, and fish, with a magnificent plate of a breaking wave (Pls. II. and III.).
3. Miners, wrestlers, dancers, negroes, various heroic figures and fantastic animals, among them a dragon-like sea-serpent.
4. Mythological heroes, birds, plants, trees, rocks, ships, men swimming and diving.
5. Architectural and mythological subjects, and a noble view of Fuji seen from the sea.
6. Archers, riders, fencers, musketeers, and wrestlers.
7. A series of magnificent landscapes with effects of storm (Pl. IV.).
8. Weavers, gymnasts, little landscapes, and caricatures of fat and thin men.
9. Subjects from history and mythology, including a noble design of soldiers marching among snow-clad mountains (Pl. V.), also some amusing pages depicting fat men.
10. Acrobats, jugglers, and some unpleasant ghosts (Pl. VI.).
11. People variously employed, wrestlers, guns and cannon.
12. The rarest of all. Caricatures.
13. Landscapes, preparations of rice, picture of an elephant's toilet, and a tiger carried down a waterfall.
14 and 15 were not published till nearly two years after Hokusai's death, and are made up from his sketches of animals.

At the risk of wearying the reader I have gone into some detail in the case of this series, because the volumes are not easy to identify without some description, and in no better way could one exhibit the vast field of inquiry upon which Hokusai entered. His aims and methods will be spoken of elsewhere; it is enough to say here that within the limits of their schemes of black, grey, and pale pink, the good things in the *Mangwa* were never surpassed, even by Hokusai himself, though the collection of his compositions published in the year of his death in three volumes, under the title of *Hokusai Gwafu*, maintains a higher average of excellence.[1] Page after page reveals designs of the greatest variety and magnificence, the simple tints of the *Mangwa* being supported in many of the plates by a printing in blue, which harmonises delightfully with the grey and coral pink. Opening a volume at random, one lights upon a great basket of flowers, the chrysanthemum, the narcissus, the iris, and the like, and on the next page we pass into a frozen marshy plain, through which a stream meanders among the deep snowdrifts, while far away a huge white mountain rises out of sight into a cold sky (Pl. XV.). Turning once more we come upon an upland path, where porters go to and fro with their burdens; by the roadside a man and a woman sit smoking, while a faggot-carrier sits on his bundle to get a light from a friend. On the next page the scene changes to the seashore, where a company of crabs of different breeds and sizes scramble about among the sand and seaweed; another turn and we are again inland among the hills at moonrise; in the hollow below runs a river, up which a man is punting a boat towards a high wooden bridge [this design, by the way, is remarkable for an attempt at drawing trees reflected in water]: while a sixth turn shows us a warrior, armed from head to foot, pausing before a palisaded cave, in which another sits sword in hand. Then come a group of fish, another landscape, a flock of birds, a beautiful group of flowers (chiefly the carnation and convolvulus), and so the series goes on, with masterpiece after masterpiece. Two other volumes, the *Santai Gwafu* and the *Ippitsu Gwafu*, published in 1815 and 1823, deserve mention from the similarity of name, but are merely collections of sketches

---

[1] This is the form in which the book is usually found. It is really a reprint of two earlier books, the *Hokusai Gwashiki* (1819) and the *Hokusai Sogwa* (1820).

recalling the less important drawings of some of the *Mangwa*, with which they are contemporary. A third book, the *Dôtchu Gwafu* (1830), is generally known, from its subject, as the *Tokaido* series. Reprints of it are common ; but, though containing some good designs, the volume is not of first-class importance.

The famous *Hundred Views of Fuji* (1834) is so well known in this country through the edition published in 1880 (London : B. T. Batsford), with an admirable commentary by Mr. F. V. Dickins, that any lengthy description of the three delightful volumes would be superfluous. The reprints, it is true, are much inferior to the early versions, but they are cheap and comparatively common, while even in worn and hastily-printed impressions the grandeur of the designs is extraordinary. Such prints as Fuji viewed through bamboos, the first upheaval of the sacred mountain, and the plate in which it rises above a grove of pine woods, on the far side of a misty river, when once seen are not easily forgotten.

The last of Hokusai's books to deserve mention are three volumes of pictures of legendary heroes—*The Personages of Suikoden* (1829), *The Heroes of China and Japan* (1836), and *The Glories of China and Japan* (1850). The first of these works is comparatively peaceful, but the two latter are packed from end to end with fierce struggling figures, conquerors of giants, demons, strange beasts, and occasionally more human enemies (Pl. XX.). In no other work does Hokusai's reverence for his Chinese predecessors show so clearly. The heroes themselves are usually Tartars ; their elaborate armour and weapons, though Japanese in design, are not drawn in the fluent Japanese manner, but with an angular realism and exact rendering of detail that is not found except in the early art of the mainland. The books seem to have given the engravers some trouble. Judging from existing sketches, Hokusai had trained men to follow with extraordinary accuracy the delicate sweeping lines that characterise his more purely Japanese work ; and in such books as the *Gwafu* very little of the spirit of the drawings was lost. With the volumes of heroes it was different. The set of finished drawings for the *Suikoden* still exists, and a glance at it shows that the change of style on the artist's part had been too much for the woodcutters. The drawings, with all their spirit,

have the cosmopolitan suavity of the most perfect naturalism—
many of the figures, indeed, are quite worthy of Rembrandt
(Pl. XIX.). In the reproductions this suavity is translated into
corners and angles and conventional black patches that reduce
the designs once more to things essentially Oriental.

So little is known about the sets and "states" of Hokusai's
large colour-prints, that it is impossible to treat them with exact
bibliographical detail. A series of five upright sheets, combining
into a big, curious picture of the interior of a *maison verte*, is
the first of these with which I am acquainted, though sheets from
still earlier books were apparently printed and sold separately.
From the style, it would seem that the *Maison Verte* was
published between 1800 and 1810. It was not till fifteen years
later that the great series of the *Thirty-six Views of Fuji*
(1823–1829), the *Bridges* (1827–1830), the *Waterfalls* (*circa*
1827), the *Hundred Poems* (*circa* 1830), and the *Flowers*, were
designed, so that these represent Hokusai's powers at their
maturity. Considerations of subject-matter interfere with the
artistic merit of some of the *Bridges*. The *Hundred Poems* are
not only rare, but very unequal. The *Thirty-six Views*, while
they contain some astonishing plates, such as "The Wave"
(Pl. XII.), the red mountain in a storm (Pl. XI.), and the red
mountain rising into a blue sky barred with cirrus cloud, do
not really maintain such a high average as the *Waterfalls*
(Pl. XIV.). In spite of much obvious convention, and a colouring
which in more than one case is powerful rather than harmonious,
the *Waterfalls* have, as a set (eight plates as known), a sustained
magnificence that even the volumes of the *Gwafu* cannot parallel.
If the one plate of the *Flowers* at South Kensington is a fair
sample of the series (Pl. IX.), the fact that it appears to be an
unique specimen is little short of a calamity, for in colour as well
as in design the bunch of chrysanthemums could hardly be more
nobly treated.

There are a good many original drawings by Hokusai in
Europe and America, but, as almost all of them are in private
hands, their study needs a certain amount of time and good luck.
Drawings made before 1810 seem to be exceedingly rare ; for out
of more than three hundred sketches which the writer has had the
opportunity of seeing, there was not one which could belong

to a period antecedent to the *Mangwa*. The sketches may be divided into two classes—drawings made for sale or display, and drawings which were studies for engraved designs. As any one acquainted with the circumstances of Hokusai's life can guess, the first class contains many sketches that are merely exhibitions of manual dexterity, without real importance. Now and then, however, there occur compositions of the utmost majesty, as in the drawing (sold in the Brinkley Collection) of two snow-clad peaks rising out of a sea of mist. The studies for engraved designs are much more interesting, but hardly the kind of thing we should expect. One imagines Hokusai's sketches to be vivid, hasty records of instantaneous impressions, rough, perhaps, but full of energy and dash. This is only the case now and then. Hokusai's methods seem to have been as deliberate as his success was complete. Again and again one comes across big studies for the little figures in the *Mangwa* and the *Gwafu*, drawn from the first with extraordinary delicacy and finish, a preliminary sketch in red often underlying the decisive work in black, but ruled across for accurate reduction, so that there may be no chance of error (Pls. VII. and VIII.). Those acquainted with fine wood-engraving know how much it may improve even good drawing,—how few of even Millais's drawings have the exquisite quality of the Dalziel cuts!—and the Japanese engravers were as skilful in their own way as Altdorfer or Lützelberger; yet when one sees Hokusai's drawings, one cannot help feeling that the engraving was really a failure, so vast is the difference between the sketches and the prints. Curiously enough, sketches for complete compositions are very rare; the studies are nearly always studies of single figures. Possibly these were only combined when drawn on to the tissue paper which was pasted on to the block, so that the original design of the whole composition was destroyed in the cutting.

A word on the current prices of Hokusai's work may not be out of place. The drawings are practically unattainable; but as the demand for them is at present small and uncertain, individual sketches, when they come into the market, do not usually fetch more than two or three guineas, that is to say, about the price of a fair print from the *Thirty-six Views*. Colour-prints or drawings of exceptional merit or scarcity may, of course, cost more. The books vary a good deal in price. When they are not printed in colours, from half a crown to ten shillings a volume, according to state, and the knowledge and nationality of the dealer, may be taken as a fair average. No price can be laid down for books of prints in colour, but if the prints are old and in good condition, a shilling a page is not unreasonable for small works. The volumes of designs for artisans have no commercial value.

Hokusai changed his signature so often that a note as to his principal *noms de pinceau* will be useful to those who wish to identify or to date his prints. These names were sometimes used alone, sometimes in combination. The signature on the prints designed when he was a pupil of Shunsho is Shunrō. In 1795 he signs Sori, and in 1796 takes the name of Hokusai (northern studio). In 1800 he adds Gwakiojin (mad about drawing) to this name, and also Tokimasa, the signature of two of the Yedo books above mentioned. In 1807 and the following years he uses the name Katsushika; in 1816, Taito; in 1820 he changes again to the name which may be read as Iitsu or Tamekadzu. From 1835 onwards he signs Manrojin or Gwakio Rojin Manji [the old man mad about drawing]. The chief of these signatures, together with those of Hokusai's best pupils, Hokuba and Hokkei, have been reproduced as an aid to identification, and will be found opposite Plate 1.

HOKUSAI—THE PAINTER OF LIFE

As the short summary of the contents of the *Mangwa* given in the previous chapter enables us to form some idea of the scope of Hokusai's studies, so the preface to the series shows us very clearly the spirit in which those studies were undertaken. "Art alone can perpetuate the living reality of the things of this world, and the only art capable of such well-doing is the true art that abides in the kingdom of genius. The rare talent of the master Hokusai is well known throughout the country. This autumn, by chance, in his journey westward, he visited our town (Nagoya), and made the acquaintance of Boksenn . . . under whose roof he dreamed and drew some three hundred compositions. The things of heaven and of Buddha, the life of men and women, even birds and beasts, plants and trees, he has included them all; and under his brush every phase and form of existence has arisen. For some time past the talent of our artists seemed to be on the wane; life and movement were lacking in their work; their hand seemed powerless to render their thought. But in the varied sketches here presented, how admirable are the sincerity and force! The master has tried to give life to everything he has painted; the joy and happiness so faithfully expressed in his work are a plain proof of his victory."

In a few words it would hardly be possible to give a better idea of Hokusai's peculiar achievement. "The things of heaven and of Buddha" alone have been enough to occupy many great painters of the East and West for a lifetime. Though naturally based on the work of his predecessors, the religious designs of Hokusai present one or two marked variations from the current artistic tradition. The masters of the Kano and Buddhist schools,

26

if not aristocrats themselves, lived with the aristocracy and regarded their art as a kind of ritual, consecrated and governed by an immemorial usage, as strict in its limitation of saintly actions and attributes as was the Spanish Inquisition. In the hands of the earlier men by whom the formulæ were first defined, the artistic impulse retained something of the freshness of youth; but in the course of several centuries of imitation, religious painting had become a thing of use and wont like the faith it embodied, and lived only by the light reflected from its past history. It had ceased to be in sympathy with popular opinion, for its conventional deities remained in a conventional heaven very far away from the realities of human existence. The Japanese, always attracted by the sensuous side of things, joined in either Buddhist or Shinto ceremonies as the taste of the moment prompted, and regarded all gods alike with a feeling of easy companionship. Hokusai was the first to give effect to this sentiment in art; indeed, in his determination to mark the links that join the immortals with mortal men, he is not afraid of caricature. The fat Hotei was half human even with the strictest of the old masters; but they never revelled in the extravagant inflation of his paunch that delighted their less reverent junior. At the same time, Hokusai was the first to make goddesses really beautiful by blending with their traditional attributes the grace and suavity of the living women around him (Pl. XVIII.). His gods, in fact, are gods of the people, who have put off their austerity and remoteness to become real and familiar comrades.

Monsters, ghosts, and demons are treated in the same spirit. They remain superhuman because it is the essence of their nature, but they are no longer misty and indefinite, or even invincible. Hokusai's dragons, for instance, are drawn with a detail of scale and claw and spine that makes their plunge from a whirl of storm-cloud seem quite a possibility. So the gigantic spider with the horrible appendages of a cuttle-fish, the fox with nine floating waving tails, the giants, and the demons are described with a nicety that, if it makes their terror less vague, makes it at the same time more actual. Yet, lest we should be frightened too much, the monsters are generally represented as getting the worst of it in their meetings with mortal heroes. The dragon drinks the nine fatal cups of *saké*, the spider is slain by the glaive of Hirai-

27

no-Hôsho, the thunder demon kneels in terror before the prodigious infant Kintoki. An exception must be made in the case of the ghosts. Hokusai's phantoms are usually very unpleasant. Even the caprices of Leonardo, Breughel, or Goya never invented anything as ghastly as the apparition of the murdered wife in the tenth *Mangwa* ; that monstrous, mutilated, idiot embryo, whose claw-like hands and single glaring eye are eloquent of irresponsible ferocity (Pl. VI.). Had the artist been cursed with the bitterness of a Salvator, he evidently could have done work of a kind it is not comfortable to think about. Fortunately Hokusai bore the world no grudge, and did not always draw ghosts.

His manner changes when he has to deal with the national heroes of China and of his own country. The grace and fluency which characterise his sketches of contemporary subjects are replaced by the decisive angularity that marks the finest Chinese naturalism, though its calm grandeur is entirely absent. Hokusai tells us the reason in one of his prefaces : " I find that in all Japanese and Chinese representations of war the force and movement which should be their essential feature are lacking. Regretting this defect, I am on fire to remedy it, and supply what was wanting." Thus it is that we see these whiskered Mongols in Japanese mail, whirled across the pages of the hero books in involved, nay extravagant, attitudes, that they may really seem to be in earnest about their sanguinary work (Pl. XX.). As before noted, the original sketches are more pleasant in effect than the prints (cf. Pls. XIX. and XX.), for the engraver has taken every opportunity of making the plates livelier than ever by black spots and masses, where the sketch is all delicate brown or grey.

The accusation of conventionalism or absurdity which might reasonably be brought against the prints of heroes, if the compositions were not so majestic, the execution so perfect, and the vigour of the movements so fresh and so unusual in a century that has apparently forgotten Rubens, fails absolutely when Hokusai comes to draw the men and women about him. His touch smooth, undisturbed, unerring, includes in its easy sweep men, women, and children in every stage of motion or rest ; noting affectionately those instinctive, momentary gestures which make action natural. With the stiff ceremonials of the court he has no sympathy, but never tires of drawing the people among whom he lived, the artisans, the shopkeepers, and country folk in all their varied amusements and employments. Actors alone he avoids. The sets of the Forty-seven Ronins are of course exceptions, but they are works of his early manhood, when perhaps a certain pride in his ancestry may have caused him to regard that one legend as something apart from the ordinary theatrical world that was so popular with his contemporaries. The humanity he really loves is for the most part a busy humanity. We see it passing briskly along the great high-roads, alert both for the incidents, the humours, and the accidents of a long journey, travelling steadily through rain and fine weather (Pl. XVI.), crossing over the drum-shaped bridges (Pls. I. and XIII.), or crammed into a ferry boat where the stream is broad or deep, wading where it is shallow (Pl. XVII.). The junks are filled with seething masses of sailors, every street view has its appropriate body of promenaders, even where we should naturally expect nothing of the kind, men are introduced, as in that winter landscape (Pl. V.), where a great army with lances and banners winds up a mountain pass; or in the picture of the great elephant, over whom his attendants are clambering while others below are rubbing him down with brushes attached to long poles.

Yet it is after all with the artisan class among whom he lived that Hokusai's sympathy is keenest. He knew by heart not only the figures of the workers and the action of their limbs, but the whole circumstance of their business and private lives, from the machines they work to their kitchen utensils. Volume viii. of the *Mangwa*, for instance, may not be particularly exciting from an artist's point of view, but a glance at it will show how thoroughly the designer was master of the details of weaving and the action of a loom. Hokusai had, in fact, the whole life of the lower class Japanese literally, at his finger tips. His attitude towards them is not that of a Millet,—for the Japanese are a cheerful race, to whom their daily toil brings no sadness,—but rather that of a Rubens, with the humour of a Daumier, and something of the feminine insight of a Watteau. He knows how men are convulsed by violent exertion, he feels the rhythmic swing of their bodies; he knows the graceful bearing of the Japanese woman, the sweeping curves of her dress,

29

the delicate fulness of her neck and limbs; he knows how children claw and crawl and waddle. Yet more than all, he knows that every motion and almost every attitude of rest has its ridiculous side; and it is this side that appeals to him. Can anything be at once more pathetic and yet more humorous than the noble composition of blind men struggling in a stream from the *Gwafu* (Pl. XVII.), where we hardly know whether to pity their helplessness or laugh at the comicality of their gestures. Nevertheless, of all painters of mirth he is the one who is least dependent upon caricature. He can of course caricature perfectly, but his mirth is too genuinely artistic, his skill of hand too perfect, his eye too accurate for exaggeration to have a permanent place in his design. His contemporaries and his pupils make their countrymen too delicately graceful or too absurdly grotesque. Hokusai alone has been able to keep the middle course, and render their comeliness and gaiety with that temperate emphasis that makes them real and living.

In animals he is quick to note character. All his beasts are full of it, from the rat (in the print room of the British Museum) nibbling the pepperpod to the furious tiger carried down the waterfall (*Mangwa*, xiii.), or the great kindly elephant. But more than all, he loves their wildness. Birds, reptiles, fishes, and quadrupeds alike cease in his hands to be the stuffed figures which even the mighty Durer or the delicate Pisanello were content to draw, but are "imperturbe, standing at ease with nature." His shaggy ponies kick and prance, his puppies sprawl, his birds scream and flirt and tumble and peck, his carp whirl in graceful curves, his dories plod along with great vacant eyes that contrast strongly with the fierce glance of some great sea marauder or the deadly fixed glare of the cuttlefish (Pl. II.). He has a special love for crabs, with their scrambling walk, their neatly-jointed plate-armour, and the double-page plate devoted to them in the *Gwafu* is one of his most successful designs. He is no scientific anatomist, he has an eye only for the outside of things, and yet he can invent animals that really seem alive. Witness the tiger among the pine needles and the curious studies, two out of several large drawings, for it (Pls. VII. and VIII.). He had to invent his tiger, since that animal is unknown in Japan. And those who are acquainted with the tiger of Japanese tradition—

that inflated tabby who never manages to look fierce — will understand how little help could come from that quarter.

He is equally at home with trees and plants. His drawings of leaves and flowers and stems in detail is as perfect as it can be (e.g. the grasses in Pl. XVI.); but in the treatment of masses of foliage he is hindered by the national custom of doing without shadow, and so his foliage in bulk becomes frankly conventional. Occasionally the convention is not a happy one. Even in careful and elaborate compositions he sometimes fails to attain that last perfection of repose which marks the noblest art, through the obtrusiveness of some too lightly suggested bough, whose scraggy proportions irritate our scientific eyes. His love of flowers differs from that of Korin or Utamaro in a preference for broadness of mass rather than the delicacy of detail, though he can work carefully enough if he chooses (Pl. IX.). He feels the spring of a bough when a bird alights upon it, or the play of curves among the blades of wind-ruffled grass. Rocks alone seem to drive him to extravagance or to the formulae of the Chinese artists who had preceded him by a thousand years. Nevertheless, his crags, if usually impossible in structure, are imposing in mass; and the comparative failure may perhaps be explained by the amorphous nature of the volcanic rocks of which the Japanese islands are in the main composed. The stones in *Mangwa* ii. are very evidently slaty crystallines of some sort, just as the cleavage of the long slab jutting into the sea in *Mangwa* vii. is quite sufficiently indicated.

His attitude is always that of the painter of aspect rather than the painter of analysis. Hence, when Hokusai deals with the nude in violent action, as in some of his large figures of wrestlers, his indication of straining muscles is not the sort of thing that would pass muster in the Academy schools; yet where he has actual experience to go upon, where he is uninfluenced by the mannerisms either of China or of his Japanese predecessors and contemporaries, the result is very different. Take, for instance, the picture of a windy day (Pl. XVI.), from the *Gwafu*, and note how the supple flesh of the girl's arms and ankles is indicated by the single sweeping line, that marks with equal accuracy and directness the masculine toughness of the next figure, and the chubby contours of the child. In drawing the

31

man's leg he has room for no more than a line to indicate the fold by the knee-cap and another for the hollow at the side of the soleus muscle, yet the limb is perfectly rendered. If this were an isolated instance one would perhaps have little right to base any claim for general recognition upon it; but when, in looking over Hokusaï's mature work, one finds evidence everywhere of the same simplicity and directness, it is impossible to deny the evidence of one's eyes and not to recognise one of the world's greatest draughtsmen. Remembering the artist's own prophecy—" When I am a hundred and ten everything I do, be it but a dot or a line, will be alive "—the statement, in the light of Hokusaï's actual achievement, is over modest, for within the limits of his materials and methods he seems to have anticipated the period of perfection by about fifty years.

HOKUSAI—THE PAINTER OF LANDSCAPE

MENTION has already been made of the geological peculiarities of Japan. The long train of islands extending nearly from the coast of Siberia to the Tropics, contains within itself almost every variety of scenery and climate, which to a certain extent is focussed, together with history, civilisation, and commerce, in the island of Nippon. Like England, this island is washed by an ocean current, and has, in consequence, a similar climate, only rather warmer and damper. Partly owing to its volcanic nature, partly owing to the fact that the whole string of islands is merely the summit of an enormous ridge, that plunges abruptly on the east into one of the deepest depressions of the Pacific, the country as a whole is mountainous, though, with the exception of Fuji and one or two others, the mountains are of no very considerable height. It is well watered by numerous rocky rivers, whose tree-clad gorges remind one of Scotland, just as certain of the seaside places at the extremity of the alluvial plains are, in the distance, not unlike some of our own watering-places. Variety of elevation and a temperate climate combine to encourage a flora of the most varied kind. The flat country, by the rivers, generally devoted to the cultivation of rice, grows plants, the bamboo for instance, that are semi-tropical or tropical; the hills are covered with pine-trees, while the gardens and roadsides are gay with cherry and plum-trees, or shadowed by cedars. The great avenues of the latter tree which line many of the now almost deserted highways are, perhaps, a more impressive reminder of bygone state than even the temples with their wonderful carvings and gay red lacquer that contrast so well with the dark foliage. The variations of the climate, the ever present mist that in warm

c 33

weather allows the distance to be visible only for a short time in the early morning, coupled with this diversity of scenery, make the country an ideal one for the landscape painter who can do no more than copy the scene before him.

Beautiful as the country is, the beauty shown in the work of its landscape artists is a different thing from the reality. Even Hiroshige, the greatest realist of them all, who draws his Fuji with the spreading cone that one sees in a photograph, in his search for the picturesque exaggerates the slopes of minor eminences, makes rocks more rugged, trees more vast, grass more green, and seas more blue. Hokusai was born some fifty years earlier, and had no forerunners but the landscapists of the Kano and Chinese schools, whose toppling precipices, jagged crags, spiky trees, and intrusive expanses of flat cloud are endlessly iterated, alike in precious *kakemono* and cheap popular guide-books. Hence it is that his early landscapes, like his early figure designs, are so coloured by tradition that to the casual eye his peculiar genius is absent. The first set of Yedo views, as we have seen, is only separated from preceding guide-books by an occasional outburst of naturalism — the river with an expanse of snow-clad fields beyond it under a dark winter sky, or the bridge with its crowd of hurrying figures. It is not until Hokusai appears in the *Mangwa* as a mature and individual artist that his landscape is really an important thing.

Even here a certain amount of progress may be traced. The first volume contains only scraps—separate sketches of varieties of trees, houses, or waterfalls ; the second, about half a dozen small and simple compositions, with a double page study of the sea (Pl. III.)—the crawling foam that creeps over the sand fold upon fold, and, below, the dark hollow of a great wave just about to break. Their juxtaposition is so ingeniously contrived that the extent, the flatness, and the complex folds of the foam enhance by contrast the massive sweep of the billow beneath. On the following pages two studies of river eddies show that the formulæ which Hokusai employed with such signal success in the *Waterfalls* were already in process of evolution. In the third *Mangwa* the few landscapes, except for another great wave, are full of Chinese convention, and show no marked advance, though a drawing of a house, made to look rather foolish by an incorrect application of the rules of perspective, shows that he was not wholly ignorant of that science. The fourth volume is again a volume of scraps; but in the fifth, after a series of careful studies of architecture, we come across a really noble landscape. Beyond an expanse of sea stretches a beach backed by a pine forest from which a wreath of white mist is driving away to the dark hills behind, and above all rise the sweeping lines of a huge snow-clad cone. Alike in accuracy of insight and quiet perfection of design the plate is in marked contrast to the other landscape in the volume, where the sea, unpleasantly frothed and twisted, drives an absurdly small boat against a tortured crag. In the seventh *Mangwa*, however, the majesty of nature is honoured more adequately (Pl. IV.). The great prints of mountains in winter rising out of the clouds over fantastic bridges, beyond the gentle lines of lesser elevations, or sweeping down into unknown space, are evidence of the labours which culminated in the landscapes of the *Gwafu* and the two sets of views of Fuji.

Our western feeling for landscape has always been rather for what is cheerful and pleasant. We admit the pensive poetry of Gainsborough or Corot, but do not at heart admire, as we ought to admire, the grander horizons of which Titian and Rembrandt give us an occasional glimpse. We fail to appreciate, except in a commercial sense, the mightiness of Turner's early maturity, the grave accomplishment of Crome, the magnificence of the Lucas mezzotints after Constable, the solemnity of Wilson, Girtin, and Cozens. These latter are of course technically imperfect, yet, the imperfection once granted, they were masters of a grandeur and simplicity which their successors never equalled. The fashionable painters of our own time are content with what is sufficiently pretty and sufficiently near to the public notion of the spots and sparkles of nature to be readily saleable. Even those whose views are more serious, whose sympathies are more profound, are content with the foreground material of the wayside. A few trees nobly arranged, a heroic barn set against a misty twilight satisfy their highest ambitions.

With Hokusai it was otherwise. As his figure-drawing embraces the whole living world known to him, so his conception of landscape includes every phase of the scenery of Japan, from the garden with its toy crags to the immensity of mountain, ocean, and wilderness. Nor does he view them only with the tranquil insight that makes his human world so gay and humorous. He is the only artist who has ever realised the majesty of winter. The grey sky of Hiroshige is bitterly cold, but his snow almost always suggests a thaw; he has a preference for the Merry Christmas side of winter weather. Hokusai knows the iron intensity of frost, as he shows by the moonlight scene among the crags in the *Gwafu*, and the terrible desolation of country buried under snowdrifts, emphasised at one time by a suggestion of utter remoteness from humanity, as in the double-peaked mountain of the seventh *Mangwa*, at another, by the introduction of man, become impotent in the face of the vast impassive nature around him, as in the scene from the *Hundred Views* (vol. iii.), where a procession with banners and trumpets passes under the great silent cone, or the print from the ninth *Mangwa*, where the straggling files of a great army wind, like ants, among snow-clad hills (Pl. V.).

Yet, while he sees that the repose of nature may be terrible (Pl. XV.), Hokusai does not forget that her motion is terrible also. We have spoken of the great wave of the second *Mangwa* (Pl. III.). With it should be compared the celebrated coloured print from the *Thirty-six Views of Fuji*, generally known as The Wave (Pl. XII.). Here once more man becomes a mere insect crouching in his frail catamaran as the giant billow topples and shakes far above him. An adherence to Chinese convention often makes Hokusai's drawing of breakers look fantastic, but they never fail of being furious—as furious as are his storms. The convention of black lines with which he represents falling rain is as effective as his conventions for water are fanciful. The storm of Rembrandt, of Rubens, or of Turner is often terrible, but never really wet; Constable gets the effect of wetness, but his storms are not terrible. Hokusai knows how a gale lashes water into foam, and bows the trees before it (Pl. IV.); how the gusts blow people hither and thither (Pl. XVI.); how sheets of driving, drenching rain half veil a landscape, and how the great white cone of his beloved Fuji gleams through a steady downpour. Clouds alone elude his simple formulæ. One or two prints in the *Mangwa* show that he made desperate efforts to master the cumulus, but the efforts were unsuccessful. The level bars of stratus he manages more easily, indeed they are part of the heritage left him by his Chinese predecessors ; and even in such a late series as the *Hundred Poems* he does not disdain to draw their thin flakes across figures and buildings in the foreground when it suits him. His lightning, too, is rather odd in comparison with the realistic studies of the great artists of Europe ; but what European ever tried an effect so stupendous as that recorded in Plate XI., where the snowy top of Fuji is seen at evening, crimson with the last fiery rays of sunset, while all the flanks of the mountain are hidden by a dark storm-cloud, through which the lightning flashes. The colours, the tones, the forms, are not perhaps those of nature, but the print is certainly magnificent, and it has yet to be proved that the thing could be done better in any other way.

Hokusai's feeling for rivers is like his feeling for mountains. He knows them well from source to sea, but has an instinctive preference for their grander aspects, the wide expanse of a reedy estuary, the massive current of the lower reaches that swings the ferry-boat this way and that, the long pools above where the stream moves gently under pine-woods, its surface dimmed by a veil of mist, and, still more, the rapids where the water whirls down among rocks and fantastic tree-trunks. Best of all, he loves the waterfall, whether it take the form of a long veil of foam sliding over the edge of a mossy precipice into some deep chasm (Pl. X.), or the downward rush of a bulkier torrent like that in which the red horse (a memory of the legend of Yoshitsune) is being washed (Pl. XIV.), or that in the plate in the thirteenth *Mangwa*, where a tiger savagely struggling is swept away into space—the terror of the plunge being suggested by the plain seen below under the arch of the falling water. No other painter has looked things in the face so frankly—has dared to express the stolid everlasting might of nature, against which scheming man and strong beast alike are powerless.

Not that man's work is wholly empty or feeble. Hokusai is not only a painter of landscape, but the painter of the life of his own country, and, as such, it is inevitable that he should deal with the landscape as modified by human effort ; the structures under which men live or worship, by which they elude or overcome the opposition of nature. He knows every joint of the complicated wooden roof of the temples (*Mangwa* v.), as well as the simpler

37

panels and frames of ordinary dwelling-houses, and uses their long simple lines to contrast with more broken and lively forms. He is especially fond of ships, from the clumsy square-built junk with its naked active sailors to the humble craft of the fisher-folk and the ferryman's punt, whose motley crowd of passengers is always as delightful to him as was the idea of the river's might eluded by man, that seems to have directed his tastes towards selecting the Bridges of Japan as a companion to his great series of *The Waterfalls* and the *Thirty-six Views of Fuji.* Apart from the opportunities of design afforded by the setting and spacing of formal architecture, he is in love with the air of dignity that these structures have when viewed from below, their great timbers rising high above the vast expanse of plain or mountain seen behind and beneath them. Even a rope bridge swinging across a chasm is made majestic by his hand, while the sacred mountain itself becomes a subordinate feature when it appears only under the water rushing from a conduit in the *Hundred Views*, struggles for supremacy with the timbers of a sluice in the *Tokaido* volume, or sinks into insignificance by the side of the gigantic beam that the sawyers are splitting in the print from the *Thirty-six Views.*

So much for the general thoughts that seem to underlie Hokusai's landscape work. The peculiarities of detail, the first thing that strike the novice, are really matters of small import-ance. His clouds, his trees, his rocks, his water, even his great mountains, are frankly conventional, and only in the two last does the convention seem quite adequate. His design often verges on the extravagant, and his topography on the impossible ; never-theless he has always the knack of giving that idea of reality, of life, which is the characteristic of his figure subjects. At first sight a composition strikes one as unnatural, but on looking into it, we find evidences everywhere of things actually seen—a row of birds pecking and chattering on a paling, odd funguses growing inside a hollow tree, a distance alive with little busy people. This exquisite insight is, indeed, characteristic of the artists of Japan. Harunobu, Koriusai, Shunsho, and Utamaro add to it extraordinary invention and delicacy of line and colour. Kiyonaga, less delicate and far less inventive than they, gained and retains popularity in virtue of his striving for realism. Hokusai stands in a place apart from them all, because he combined with this insight a majesty of design, a seriousness of purpose, and a comprehension of the true relation between man and nature, that even Western art has yet to parallel. That his true greatness has sometimes to be read between the lines of his work, is the result of nationality and circumstance, of technical limitations, for which proper allowance is not usually made. Space does not allow of their being discussed at great length, but the few notes given in the following chapter may at least serve to prevent misunderstanding.

CHARACTERISTICS OF HOKUSAI'S WORK

As the reader will have already surmised, by far the larger portion of Hokusai's handiwork consists of brush drawings in black and white for engraving on wood. He left a great number of paintings, but these are for the most part so inferior to his engraved designs that they deserve no mention here. They were probably "pot-boilers," painted to supply some pressing need, for they are frequently hasty in handling and fortuitous in arrangement.

In considering the engraved designs, we have to realise, in the first place, the limitations under which they were produced. National tradition prohibited the introduction of shadow, but this prohibition would have had little weight with an independent spirit like that of Hokusai. His own words, already quoted, prove that he had seen how, by shadow, the Europeans produce a deceptive imitation of nature, but he adds that the Japanese artist is content with form and colour. That the most truly decorative painting of the West, from Giotto to Puvis de Chavannes, has in practice limited itself in a similar way is a warning against condemning Hokusai's choice too hastily.

We have again to remember that it was the national custom to draw with the brush instead of with the pen, which accounts for certain peculiarities of technique. Nevertheless, in Hokusai's hands, the brush has none of the disabilities of the stiffer instrument; indeed, a drawing of a Chinese warrior in the writer's possession is done with such extraordinary exactness and freedom, that even Dürer would have found it difficult to copy.

Again, all Japanese drawing is done in black on a white ground. They thus miss the brilliant effects obtained by

40

engravers, who design in white on black; and Hokusai is no exception to the rule. His design is blonde in general effect, and, except in fine early impressions, the darks are apt to look spotty, through over-printing, by contrast with the light portions. As has already been mentioned, the plates in the hero books suffer terribly in this respect.

When due allowance has been made for these peculiarities, it at once becomes evident how magnificent a draughtsman Hokusai is. His hand is so steady that he can draw like a machine; his knowledge is so complete, that he can get straight to reality with the directness of a Rembrandt; his early work shows that he can imitate the feminine airs and graces of his predecessors; his later, that he had the secret of the vigour and force of the great Chinese masters. His skill is limited only by the shores of his native island, for, as we have seen, he drew most of its contents that were worth the drawing. He was master of the life and movements of the men and beasts around him, as no other artist has ever mastered the animate world of his own country. Besides drawing real things, he could design the unreal, and has created ghosts and monsters with a spirit and individuality that are quite unparalleled. He has the misfortune to be a humorist as well, so that his inimitable caricatures, his tendency to the attitude of the laughing philosopher, have given him, with the shallow and the ill-informed, the reputation of being merely the funny man of Japan. He draws the largest mass as magnificently as he draws the tiniest detail. His hand treats the great curves of wave or mountain, the sweeping folds of a dress, as accurately and easily as he draws the turn of an eye or a mouth, the gesture of a finger, or the engraving on a sword hilt.

Yet, with all his natural gifts, he was too much devoted to his art to run the risk of failure through negligence. His whole history is a record of eager, unceasing study, and those who have looked over any considerable collection of his drawings will begin to realise that even a heaven-born genius does not achieve great success without great labour. In one collection alone, four large studies three or four times the size of the engraving exist for the print of the tiger jumping through a dust of leaves and pine needles in *Mangwa* xiii. The two here reproduced (Pls. VII. and VIII.) show how carefully Hokusai considered the form of the beast as well as his hide, and how he ruled his sketches across to ensure accurate reduction. When we remember that this volume appeared in the year of his death, and that the studies were therefore made when his powers were in their fullest maturity, we can form some slight idea of the incalculable amount of preparatory labour on which the vast engraved output of his life must have been based. That there is not a trace of this toil in his completed work is, perhaps, the most remarkable feature of Hokusai's success.

His colour cannot be praised so unreservedly. During his youth and early manhood the colour instinct of the Japanese popular painters reached its climax in the hands of Harunobu, Hokusai's own master Shunsho, and Utamaro. The climax was as shortlived as it was extraordinary, for by the beginning of the nineteenth century Japanese colour had fallen from its supreme perfection of elaborate harmony to the vulgar violence of Toyokuni and his followers. Hokusai, who had imitated Shunsho and Utamaro with considerable success while their influence was predominant, had too much independence to rush to the opposite extreme when it became fashionable. The greens and crimsons and purples that clash so violently in the work of Toyokuni were subdued and modified by him till they ceased to be discordant, and combine into harmonies that are certainly pleasant if not exactly noble. It was not, however, till the revolt against popular convention was made a certain success by the publication of the *Mangwa* that he ventured upon the elaborate prints in colour on which his fame of to-day rests.

Compared with the efforts of his contemporaries, with the occasional exception of Hiroshige, the result is masterly; yet it will not stand comparison in every respect with the best work of eighteenth-century Japan any more than his drawing, just because it is not conventional, quite catches certain delicate graces of Utamaro's best work. The colours in Hokusai's five great series —the *Thirty-six Views*, the *Bridges*, the *Waterfalls*, the *Flowers*, and the *Hundred Poems*—are delightful from their frankness and purity rather than from any complex subtlety. From his treatise on colouring it is evident that the quality of the pigments he used was the matter which interested him most; and it is therefore exceedingly important that he should be judged only by fine old proofs and not by the modern reprints now so common, in which the colours are coarse and muddy.

The result of his simple tastes is evident in all his finer plates. The combinations and contrasts of colour are quite in harmony with the characteristic features of his design—at once fresh and massive, though his preference for a hot, ferreous red is apt to be rather overwhelming when it is not contrasted with a corresponding amount of cool pigment. If Plate XI. be compared with Plate XIV. it will be seen how, in the case of the mountain scene, the masses of deep blue are strong enough to balance the hot colour, while, in the case of the waterfall, the red rocks are unduly predominant. It should be added, in fairness to Hokusai, that the latter proof, though old, is not in all probability one of those printed under his immediate supervision. At the same time, his paintings show clearly enough that in later life this taste for hot colour became habitual. After all, it is only because Hokusai is one of a nation of colourists that his gifts in this respect seem limited. How few works, for instance, of our own water-colour school could be placed beside his prints without looking weak or crude or dirty? Though he fails to equal such men as Harunobu or Utamaro in certain respects, it is because in those respects Harunobu and Utamaro are supreme, and because they paid for their supremacy by sacrificing almost everything else to it.

If the Japanese are by nature a nation of colourists, they are a nation of designers as well, and designers with a very marked aptitude for exquisite grace and delicacy, but perhaps rather too happy and facile to achieve the majestic. Among the earlier artists, the lacquerer Korin alone seems to have stiffened the sweetness of his country with a proportionate measure of strength, though occasionally the Kano school in their imitation of Chinese design chance upon some dignified motive. During the first forty years of his life Hokusai is Japanese to the core, graceful, fluent, versatile, capricious, but rarely grave or grand. The enthusiastic industry that made him, as we have seen, a student in turn of all the available styles of art, led in due course to an imitation of Korin and then of the painters of the mainland. Now, as far as art was concerned, China was to Japan what Egypt was to Greece—the square, massive masculine element that gave to the fluent, lively graces of the maritime nation the grit and backbone that it needed. Hokusai was not slow to realise this. The first result of the new knowledge was the blending of sweetness with power that makes the figures of the *Mangwa* so precious. By 1830, when his enthusiasm for land-scape was at its height, the Chinese influence had become part of his being, till, when he worked upon the hero books, his design has an angular force through which Japanese graces peep but rarely. As the peculiarities of their execution in these latter cannot be examined without a study of the mannerisms of Chinese painting, there is no space to discuss them adequately here. It will therefore be best to confine our attention to the design of Hokusai's middle period, when the characteristics of the main-land and of the artist's own island are most perfectly blended.

Europe has so long been dominated by the sober ideas of composition that are associated with the names of Raphael and Claude that it has still to become accustomed to the less restrained balance of form and colour that pleases the Oriental eye. We are apt to pity Rembrandt and to despise Goya when they are original enough to pass beyond the limits imposed by academic pedants, so that we are hardly ready to view fairly the more constant divergence of the Japanese. Yet it is undeniable that the old formulæ have produced nothing but dulness and pomposity with all but the greatest of our artists. The very moderation that the balancing of one thing by another implies, the search for a succession of points of interest, do not really make for strength but for weakness. The tendency of minds with no definite original purpose is to touch up all subordinate objects till they cease to be subordinate, and the main point gets lost in a tangle of competing interests. Even Hokusai is occasionally so fond of some small detail of gesture or character that he is apt to make it unduly obtrusive, but rarely so far as to interfere with the real central thought. Anyone who examines even the few compositions reproduced in this volume will be able to tell at a glance the real motive underlying them. A great wave, a great waterfall, a great bridge, a great mountain, a great figure,— whatever he wants to emphasise,—he sees without a distracting environment, and means that there shall be no doubt about it. His design, in fact, instead of being eccentric is unusually direct and simple.

This simplicity, this avoidance of anything like equal quantities, really lies at the root of Hokusai's artistic dignity. When he wishes to make anything look high he places it high up on the page, not only because this conveys the impression of its being far above the spectator's horizon, but also because an exceedingly unequal division of the page at once attracts attention to the larger mass.

So he conveys the impression of space, and suggests a vast environment, unseen in the actual picture, by letting the lines of the composition run out of it freely so that they appear to be unlimited, in contrast to the Western notion that everything must be strictly confined within the picture space, and that the corners must be rounded off or merged in shadow. If a study of Hokusai did no more than deal the deathblow of the vignette, that emasculate heresy which has for two centuries been the refuge of the tradesman and the dunce, it would confer upon European painters the boon that they need most.

Hokusai's taste for Chinese methods often leads him into an imitation of their forcible angular handling that tends to make individual parts of his work look fussy. Fortunately he combines with this taste the national love for exquisitely spaced straight lines and long sweeping contours, that form its most perfect complement. Indeed, in the hands of his predecessors, the harmonies of gentle curves and straight lines were become as languid as their colour, and Hokusai's jagged brush-work was just what was wanted to revive the national style. European painters too often design with small curves, and have only half understood that the perfect spacing of straight lines which makes fine architecture or fine furniture can also go a long way towards making fine pictures. Anyone who has studied the more abstract side of the art of Greece or of pre-Raphaelite Italy will see, if he only looks carefully enough, that the principles underlying such a design as that in the second volume of the *Hundred Views*, where Fuji is seen behind the vertical lines of a dyer's goods hung out to dry, are identical with those that were felt by the great vase painters and by Donatello. As one turns over the leaves of the volume, and comes across design after design all wonderful, and all utterly distinct from each other, it is impossible not to be struck by the hopelessness of attempting to explain more than the one

45

or two points that force themselves most definitely on the mind. Reproductions, however carefully done, always interpose a screen of some kind between artist and spectator. In the case of bad painters this is an advantage ; in the case of great men it can never be anything but a misfortune. Unluckily, fine Japanese prints, owing to the yellowish tone of the paper, defy photography, so that the little engravings annexed can convey only a slight idea of their originals. Only by actual examination of the master's work can any idea be formed of the extraordinary variety of experiments which he turns into triumphs. So universal, indeed, is the achievement of Hokusai, that the painter who can learn nothing from a careful study of his prints must either be unfit for his trade, or a greater genius than any the world has hitherto known.

ILLUSTRATIONS

春郎	宗理	北斎	辰政	葛飾
i	ii	iii	iv	v
載斗	卍老人	爲一	北溪	北馬
vi	vii	viii	ix	x

SIGNATURES OF HOKUSAI AND HIS PUPILS

i. SHUN-RÔ.
ii. SÔ-RI.
iii. HOK-USAI.
iv. TOKI-MASA.
v. KATSU-SHIKA.

vi. TAI-TO.
vii. MAN-RO-JIN.
viii. IIT-SU OR TAMEKAD-SU.
ix. HOK-KEI.
x. HOK-UBA.

PLATE II

PLATE III

PLATE IV

PLATE V

累ね
怨魂

祐天和尚

PLATE VI

Plate VII.

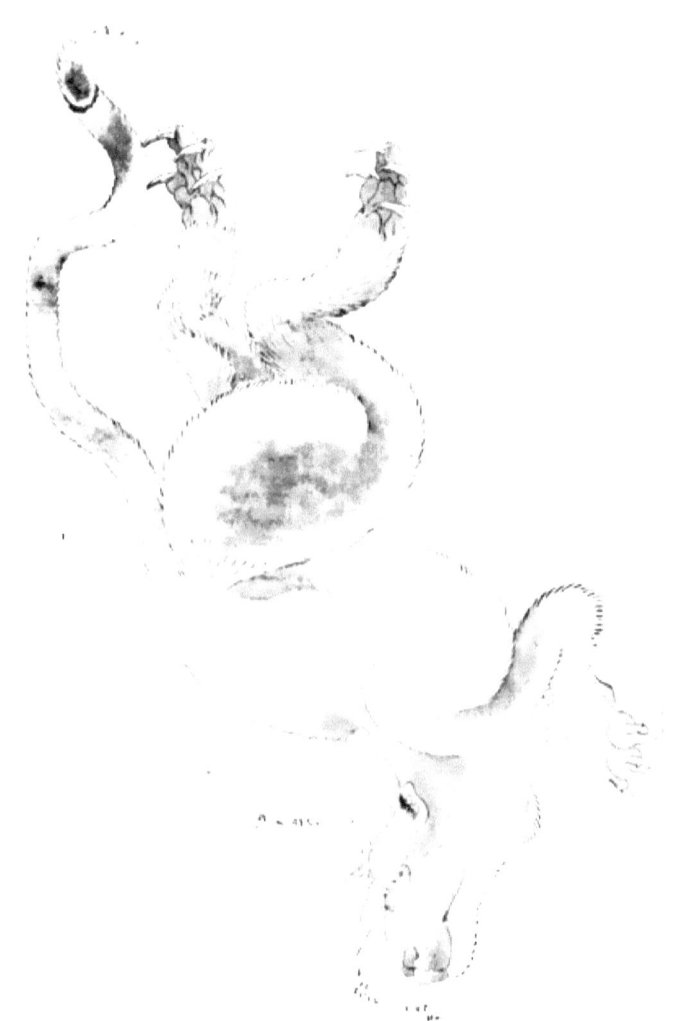

PLATE VIII

PLATE IX

PLATE X

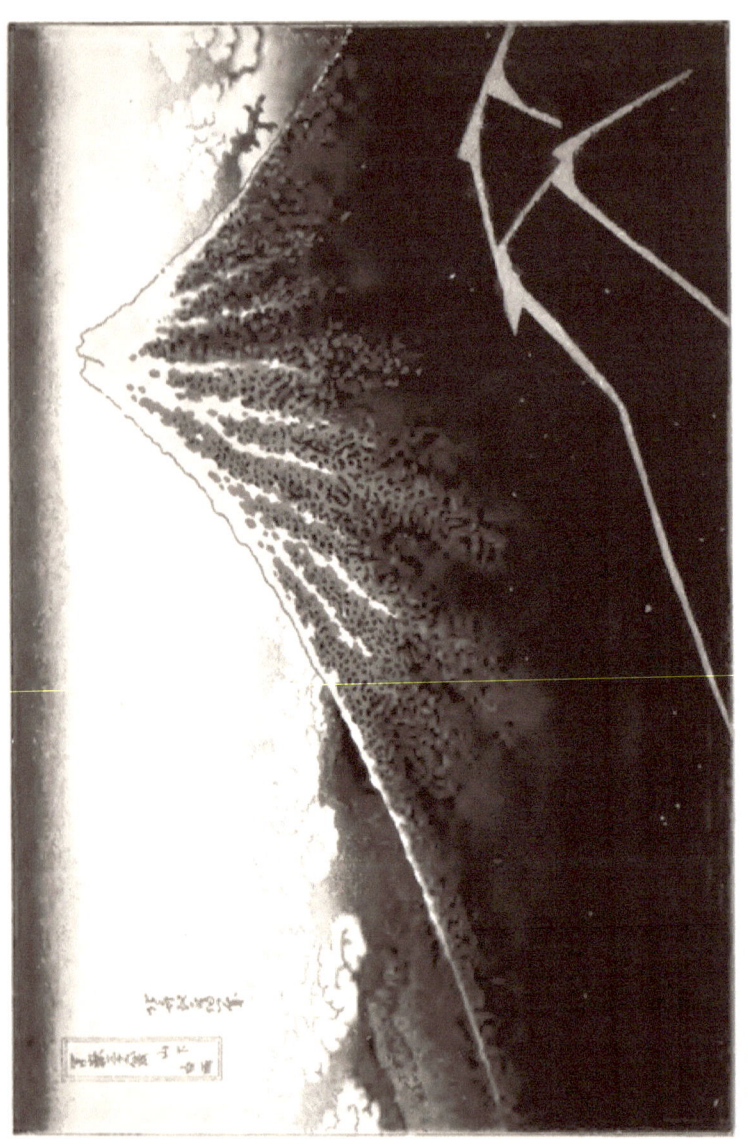

Pl. XII.

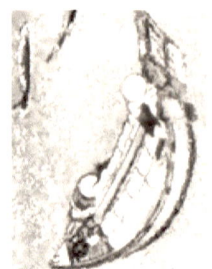

PLATE XV

PLATE XVI.

PLATE XVII.

PLATE XVIII

PLATE XIX.

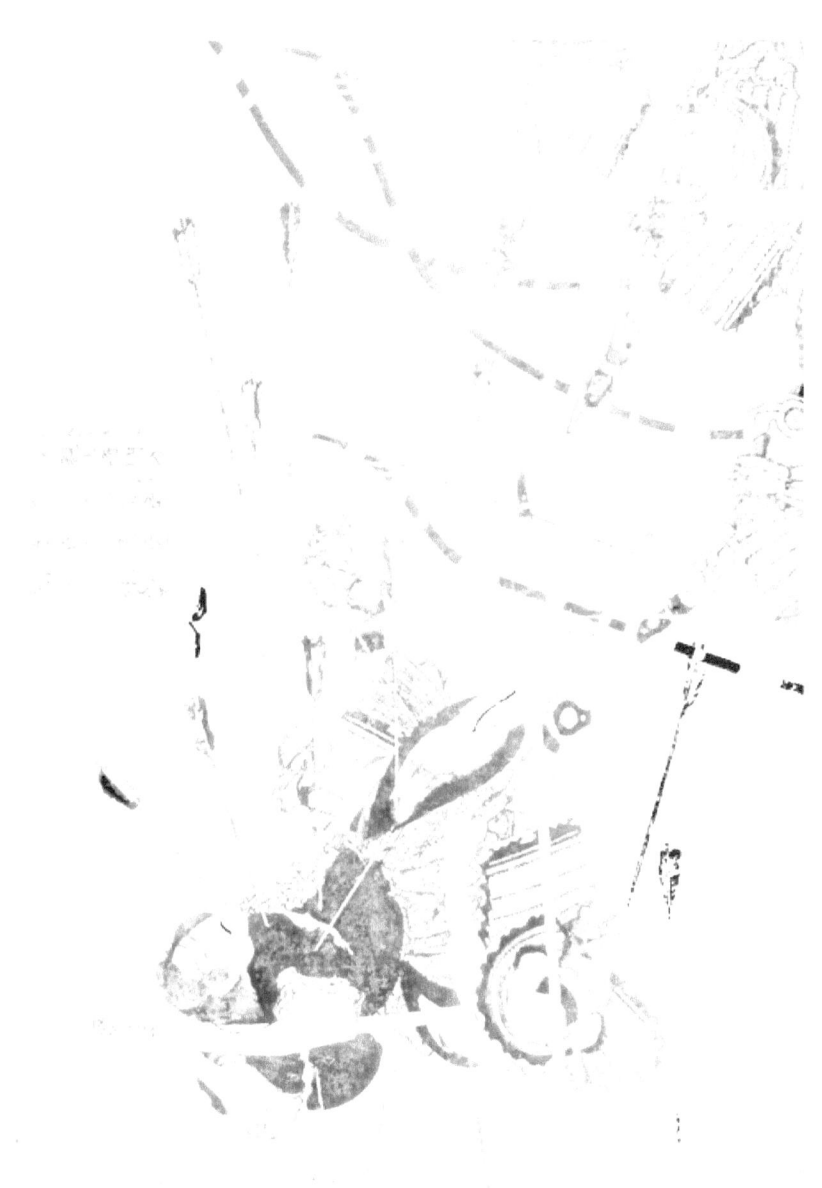